Everything You Touch

Sheila Callaghan

A SAMUEL FRENCH ACTING EDITION

SAMUEL FRENCH

FOUNDED 1830

SAMUELFRENCH.COM
SAMUELFRENCH-LONDON.CO.UK

MUSIC USE NOTE

Licensees are solely responsible for obtaining formal written permission from copyright owners to use copyrighted music in the performance of this play and are strongly cautioned to do so. If no such permission is obtained by the licensee, then the licensee must use only original music that the licensee owns and controls. Licensees are solely responsible and liable for all music clearances and shall indemnify the copyright owners of the play(s) and their licensing agent, Samuel French, against any costs, expenses, losses and liabilities arising from the use of music by licensees. Please contact the appropriate music licensing authority in your territory for the rights to any incidental music.

IMPORTANT BILLING AND CREDIT REQUIREMENTS

If you have obtained performance rights to this title, please refer to your licensing agreement for important billing and credit requirements.

EVERYTHING YOU TOUCH was first presented at the Theatre at Boston Court in Pasadena, California in a co-production with Rattlestick Playwrights Theater on April 2, 2014. The performance was directed by Jessica Kubzansky, with sets by Francois-Pierre Couture, costumes by Jenny Foldenauer, lights by Jeremy Pivnick, props by John Burton, original composition and sound by John Zalewski, and video by Adam Flemming. The Production Stage Manager was Jenny Smith. The cast was as follows:

VICTOR	Tyler Pierce
JESS	Kirsten Vangsness
LEWIS	Arthur Keng
MODELS	Allegra Rose Edwards, Chelsea Fryer, Candice Lam
ESME	Kate Maher
LOUELLA	Amy French

EVERYTHING YOU TOUCH received its New York premiere at Rattlestick Playwrights Theater on January 28, 2015 in a co-production with Theatre at Boston Court. The performance was directed by Jessica Kubzansky, with sets by Francois-Pierre Couture, costumes by Jenny Foldenauer, lights by Jeremy Pivnick, props by John Burton, original composition and sound by John Zalewski, and video by Adam Flemming. The Production Stage Manager was Theresa Flanagan and the Assistant Stage Manager was Rachael Gass. The cast was as follows:

VICTOR	Christian Coulson
JESS	Miriam Silverman
LEWIS	Robbie Tann
MODELS	Allegra Rose Edwards, Chelsea Fryer, Nina Ordman
ESME	Tonya Glanz
LOUELLA	Lisa Kitchens

This play was originally commissioned by and developed with True Love Productions in New York City. Further development and support was provided by the Creativity Fund at New Dramatists."

CHARACTERS

VICTOR

JESS

LEWIS

MODELS

ESME

LOUELLA

FEMALE VOICE

AUTHOR'S NOTES

Throughout the play, the chorus of models will be used as furniture, wallpaper, lamps, decor, often in a humorous way, However, this occurs ONLY in the scenes that feature Jess. Also, let it be noted – when not parading around the imagination of Jess or in a literal fashion show, they are ever-present objects, to be objectified at will.

Act Titles are projected throughout.

SPECIAL THANKS

The playwright would like to thank the following people, without whose guidance, insights, talents, and support this would not exist: Kip Fagan, Emily Morse, John Steber, Erin Deitrick, Todd London, Jason Grote, Dan Deitz, Rinne Groff, Zakkiah Alexander, New Dramatists, Katie Meister, Michael Tisdale, Polly Lee, Seth Glewen, Danielle Slavick, Danyon Davis, Leeanne Hutchison, Adam Greenfield, Jessica Kubzansky, Michael Seel, Michael Michetti, Hillary Metcalf, Cheryl Rizzo, Brian Polak, Emilie Beck, Aaron Henne, Jeanne Donovan Fisher, Laurie Gilmore, Eve Zappulla, Mandy Freund, Kirsten Kollander, Scott Lowell, Kellen Law, Andrea Thome, Tamilla Woodward, Aya Cash, Kate Decoste, Bhavesh Patel, Daoud Heidami, Sam Reisman, Ramon Deocampo, Dorie Barton, Adam Hunter, Emily Kosloski, Heidi Schreck, David Van Asselt, May Adrales, Dan Halsted, and perhaps most importantly, Tom Cole. And a final hat-tip to Jon Kern for assistance with any and all ass-jokes.

PROLOGUE

Piper

(As the house lights dim, **JESS** *walks across the theatre onto the stage. She is dressed like a slob. Her hair is unwashed, her skin is greasy, her posture is slumped. She grips a coffee mug. She is miserable. Maybe she scratches her ass. Looks around at her shitty surroundings. Then vanishes offstage.)*

(Slam. Lights up on 1974.)

(Projected: "**VICTOR CAVANAUGH**, *Spring 1974")*

(We witness an amazing fashion show. The **MODELS** *totter in wearing their furs, leathers, and animal prints. Extravagant, theatrical, perverse, treacherous, gothic, avant garde.)*

(The final model struts down the runway. She trips and falls.)

(Lights up on **VICTOR** *talking to the model who fell. He is skinny, odd, dramatic. He chainsmokes.)*

VICTOR. Piper

I am tired of your pretty, lyrical, thought-provoking face.

When I'm sitting elbow to elbow at a runway show

I want to see what television and film and a book and poetry can't deliver.

Immediacy. Fervor. Wreckage.

VICTOR. *(cont.)* When the model spits with rage, I want to feel that spittle.

I want to smell your sweat.

I want to taste your bile.

I want my blood to boil.

And I want to feel too overwhelmed after the experience to speak.

This, to me, is the power of fashion.

It's ugly.

It's furious.

It creeps into my thoughts long after I've gone.

That's why I design.

I make clothes that are obsessive, anxiety-ridden, fast-talking.

I don't make antiques.

I don't sew for history books.

I love confusion.

I love to watch people flail with passionate intention.

I love to watch bodies fabricate themselves.

This is life.

It's a grotesque, furious, freakish pageant.

> *(The* **MODEL** *looks away.* **VICTOR** *snaps his fingers in her face.)*

Pay attention please.

I see my profession as

the fraught dialogue of a naked woman with all the hexes and spells of my fabric

It's a lover's quarrel that ends in murder

Piper.

Piper.

Are you listening to me?

Are your big blinking eyes soaking this in?

Do you know what inspires me?

Poverty.

Terrible terrible poverty.
I spent time in Guatemala
They exist on avocados
They live in shacks with tin roofs
Buildings crumbling apart
Naked babies squatting in the road
Donkeys
But even there in the muck of mortal despair
There's an indefatigable humanity
It claws from the depths of pure anguish
THAT inspires me
THAT is what drives my impulses
THAT is what feeds my soul.
THAT is what you lack.

You are not a ruin.
You are youth and sex and butter
But I want gristle and grime.
Barbaric elegance.

You, Piper.
You are not visionary
You are not fearless
You do not have immense volume
Nor are you idiosyncratic.
You don a long-sleeved blouse and say "Wait! I can't see
   my watch!"
When you should be saying, "Why would I need a time
   piece? When I wear this garment, time STOPS."

The person I'm looking for slumbers on a metal grate
Under a tarp of nails
And eats leather and roots and feces

Can you make the sound of an ambulance siren with
   your pupils?
Can you wear a steel cage like it's heat-crinkled silk
   organza?

Can you make a garment look like a Sunday suicide?
No. No no no.

So.

Where does that leave us?

> *(The* **MODEL** *vanishes.)*

> *(Then. In silhouette. We see the* **MODEL** *commit suicide.)*

PART ONE

Fuck You Fuck You

(*JESS appears in her office. She is lit by the glow of her computer screen.*)

(**LEWIS** *hangs over her shoulder. Both wear drab clothes. They are colored sickly beneath the fluorescent lights.*)

(*The* **MODELS** *are the desks, the chairs, the bad art on the walls.*)

JESS. *(to us)* I hit the down arrow on my keyboard hard several times. I am aware the force of my finger is excessive but I am still meekly satisfied by this gesture… With my other hand I raise my coffee cup to my lips, knowing the coffee is terrible cold and also knowing it was terrible when it was hot. The coffee reminds me I am not made of pixels and page hits. I am capable of feeling wetness. I am human.

> *(to* **LEWIS**)

Okay. The overview is fine. The 'scope of work' is fine… You spent a lot of time on this.

LEWIS. Yeah.

JESS. *(reading)* Sowuuuuuuhhhhhhhh underlying architectural changes that will be implemented during this project right right right right future initiatives will be easier to implement and ultimately become more scalable God who the fuck told them we'd be done with this mess by December? Seriously?

LEWIS. We all decided that.

JESS. In the past three years they've done so many work-arounds and patch-ups it'll take five months just to slash through it. Did you talk to Lisa directly?

LEWIS. Yes.

JESS. *(to us)* I become aware that several clumpy pieces of my unwashed hair are stuck to the eyelashes of my right eye. I realize I haven't showered in four days. I wonder if Lewis can smell the oil of my scalp.

LEWIS. You smell weird. I think Lisa has someone who knows HTML.

JESS. H T Fucking M L. You're serious.

LEWIS. No.

JESS. You're joking.

LEWIS. Have you eaten lunch yet?

JESS. No.

> (**LEWIS** *stands and grabs the strap of the brown leather messenger bag from the back of* **JESS**'s *chair, which may or may not be a* **MODEL**. *He hands the bag to* **JESS**.)

LEWIS. Beep beep beep. Burrito intervention. Let's go.

> (*They are now in a burrito place… A bassy African groove plays loudly above.* The* **MODELS** *are now Chipotle furnishings, food, and etc.*)

JESS. *(to us)* Chipotle's is crammed full of broody office clothing with humans speaking in decibels several notches louder than hospitable. *(to* **LEWIS***, spotting a chair, loudly)* Oh oh oh, get it get it! (**LEWIS** *grabs a chair*) I pinch at the folds of fat hanging over my waistband and apologize to my body in advance for what I am about to ingest.

> *(to* **LEWIS***)*

This place has a way of making you feel one rung lower in the cultural food chain.

LEWIS. What do you mean?

JESS. The music is globally responsive, the patrons are coiffed, and all the brushed metal trimmings and

exposed ductwork and blond wood and track-lighting…
it's like you're not just buying a sub-par Mexican meal,
you're buying a lifestyle.

LEWIS. What are you talking about.

JESS. I'm just tired of the assumption that I need a chain
restaurant to tell me who I am.

LEWIS. It's all natural farm fresh ingredients, Jess. You can
stand to be awash in modernity for that.

JESS. *(to us)* He doesn't know about the email I got this
morning from my mother's neighbor. An elderly
woman with one good eye, two good teeth, and posture
like an elbow macaroni.

> *(The* **MODELS** *circle* **JESS**. *They speak in unison.
> It's eerie.)*

MODELS. You are so beautiful, Jess. And so *skinny*. Were you
walking around in Mommy's high heels this morning?

JESS. Yes.

MODELS. You little peanut. Do you want me to buy you a
new dress?

JESS. Yes.

MODELS. You are about a million times prettier than the
other girls in your kindergarten class. I feel bad for
them.

JESS. Me too.

> *(***JESS** *stabs the center of her burrito and shoves a
> forkful into her mouth. The* **MODELS** *become the
> decor a moment.)*

GNNAGGGKKK…

> *(She grasps her paper cup and begins sucking
> urgently at the straw.)*

LEWIS. Why get the hot sauce if you can't handle it?

JESS. I need to suffer for my food.

LEWIS. You need some time off. Chill for a week. Go to
a spa. Do some yoga. Take some shrooms. Have a
spiritual awakening.

JESS. My mother is dying.

> *(Beat. The* **MODELS** *lean in slightly.)*

LEWIS. Really?

JESS. Yeah.

LEWIS. Should you go be with her?

JESS. Unclear.

> *(They freeze/disappear.)*

> *(Lights up on* **VICTOR** *and* **ESME** *in the '70s in* **VICTOR***'s boutique. They are smoking.* **ESME** *fusses with a gumball machine. She is a slim female protégé with a feathered haircut from the '70s and tons of black eyeliner. She is gorgeous and full of drama. She holds herself just so.)*

VICTOR. Suicide.

Really?

That is the most BANAL choice a human can make.

The world is maybe better off without such a BANAL choice-maker.

I didn't invent truth you know.

Should I have said "YES! PERFECTION! THANK YOU!

"You shit rubies and I want to eat them."

Her one job in life is to walk in a straight line

Point A to point B.

One foot then the other then the other then the other then... Done.

She failed.

Not my fault, am I right?

ESME. Also her ass was huge

VICTOR. I mean did you see that?

Should have its own zip code.

Fucking fuck.

There was more press about the suicide than the clothes

Did anyone even see the clothes?

> *(***ESME** *grabs a newspaper and reads.)*

ESME. September 10, 1974. Victor Cavanaugh, a local designer with a small but fierce following, has presented a Spring line that is garishly delectable, and his solid/architectural

VICTOR. "It's all UN-FUCKING-WEARABLE."

>   *(then)*

So she couldn't walk, so what! Must be a hundred other jobs in this city for tiny women with saucer eyes and weak ankles. I shouldn't have said any of that stuff to her. I was imitating a self that no longer exists.

ESME. *(calming)* Shhhhh. Where are the matches?

VICTOR. Over there.

>   **(ESME** *grabs matches and lights a lavender candle.)*

ESME. Landlord is still burning that filthy sulfur oil. Makes everything smell like boiled eggs.

VICTOR. I stopped noticing.

ESME. 'Cause you never leave the store.

VICTOR. I want to *see* my customers. I want to understand who is interested in what I make. If anyone. I don't feel well, Esme.

ESME. Fine, I'll pull for tomorrow and you can spit some ideas for Fall.

VICTOR. I have none.

ESME. Don't make me pity fuck you. I'm too high right now.

VICTOR. You're high?

ESME. That dead model had a hippie boyfriend who passed out dime bags before the show. Speaking of chumps, we're supposed to get some bunny shipped in this week from like, Little Rock.

VICTOR. Why is she coming *here?*

ESME. For that promotion we did with the NBC radio affiliate. VIP fashion treatment. Tour of your workroom and maybe a free headband. You said you wanted more attention from the middle.

VICTOR. I said I wanted the mainstream to catch on to my ideas. As in, have them make their way to me on their own. Not yank them from their sofas and ram my designs down their gullets.

ESME. Some folks need to be bludgeoned into awareness. What's that quote, "fashion must be the axe for the frozen sea inside us"?

VICTOR. That's Kalfka. He was talking about literature.

ESME. Art is art.

VICTOR. Art is shit. Who wears a fucking nine thousand dollor jacquard chiffon blazer cut for someone six-foot-three and ninety-two pounds? In the worst fucking economy since the depression? As if the Sixteenth Century will *ever* come back into fashion?

> *(He begins arranging the jackets on the rack.)*

They are stunning, though. If I'd gotten my start in the '60s I'd be ten years younger and a household name. Not drowning in a sea of F.I.T. infants in their parent-funded shops. You spit.

ESME. So the other day? I'm thinking about Vietnam, right? And I get this vision.

> *(She reveals something distinct and representative of the line she imagines, which will absolutely be remembered when it emerges again later on in the play.)*

A G.I. Jezebel cabaret show

Military tailcoats

metal-epaulettes

shrapnel holes

Rusty bullet belts

sequined camos

And…septum rings made of hanging garnets!

Nosebleed chic!

These bitches will fight for our love

Because our love is war, man

What do you think?

VICTOR. I think it's gonna piss a lot of people off.

ESME. It could be our fall line. The troops will be out by then. And even if they aren't – it's protest art! Co-opting the bloody spectacle and cranking it through the glamourizer. You don't think the kids will eat that shit up?

VICTOR. I think the kids a) couldn't afford it and b) are tired of the war being commodified and sold back to them.

ESME. I got a feeling about this –

VICTOR. Is that pity-fuck still on the table?

> *(ESME drops her panties and bends over the work table in her dress.)*

ESME. Don't get me sweaty. I want to wear this to the Missoni dinner tonight.

> *(Freeze on them.)*

> *(Lights up on JESS in a bar. Alone. The MODELS are the bartender, the bar, the neon beer sign.)*

JESS. *(to us)* My mother is dying

My mother is dying

I say it over and over

Waiting to feel something

Nothing comes

So

Instead of purchasing an economy seat

On a budget airline to the South

To watch a dying woman who hates me

Take sips of oxygen

From a nose tube

I'm waiting for someone I haven't met yet.

We don't have an appointment.

He may not even exist.

But here are his stats:

One.

He is skinny
The kind of skinny that makes people nervous
It's partially genetic
But mostly he just smokes a lot
And forgets to eat
I'm so jealous of that.

Two.
He wears gorgeous clothes.
Clothes I've only seen in photos.
The kind I could never bring myself to buy.
He spends every penny he makes on them
He'd rather be poor than have an unfit garment touch
    his skin
But he isn't superficial
He just loves himself
Some people do.

Three.
He looks like my father.
Who died when I was two so I can't call upon his face
with any precision but that's probably okay 'cause now
I can make my small inventions around the parts I do
know such as his body type, his complexion, his hairline.

Four.
He'll have no qualms about allowing a tipsy degenerate
to take him home.

Five.
We're gonna have some crazy epic drunk sex. Slamming
against walls and tearing up bedsheets, et cetera.
Someone will probably get a black eye. It'll go on for
like, ever. And eventually his particles will become mine
and we'll shrink down all microscopic. We'll travel into
the corpuscles of strangers, in and out of cells and cilia,
through mucous membranes, beneath fingernails, then
out into the earth, through the roots of a grass blade,
through the hard shells of Amazonian insects, onto

the tongues of termites, and oh then we'll get fucking HUGE! We'll billow upwards into the galaxy and cloak the constellations, wrap 'em up like wedding gifts. And then we'll collapse in the pull of our own gravity and reconstitute as a white, heatless star, and wash the universe in our ghostly glow.

Yeah, man.

That's how rockin' our sex will be.

Six.

This is more me than him but he'll fall asleep right after and I'll just stroke him and talk to his sleeping body like people do on TV.

I'll tell him this:

"I am stroking the space between your ear and your shoulder

"I am stroking the space between your hip and your thigh

"I am stroking the space between your spine and your navel

"I am consumed with your spaces between"

And from these I'll build out my father. Shape him from dust and aromas and smoke and breath and everything else in the invisible world.

And later on I'll wonder if I raised my father from the dead just so I could fuck him.

Which is pretty dark, right?

But

First he's gotta walk through that door.

> (**VICTOR** *walks through the door, looking much as described. He wears gorgeous clothes. He immediately lights a cigarette.*)

VICTOR. Hey.

JESS. Hey.

VICTOR. Pretty dead in here

JESS. All the hipsters are across the street doing '90s
karaoke

That's a hell of a jacket

VICTOR. It's really fucking hot out

But I can't take it off

It's a perfect reflection of my id right now

JESS. You look thirsty

Can I buy you a drink?

VICTOR. Don't you want my name first?

JESS. Not a requirement.

VICTOR. Fair enough. Dry martini please. With a twist.

JESS. Not really a man's drink.

VICTOR. I'm not really a man.

I'm a filthy, bratty, terrible baby.

JESS. Nice sales pitch.

VICTOR. Something tells me you don't need the hard sell

(The **MODEL** *serves him his drink.)*

What do you do?

JESS. I work for an upstart dotcom. I dream in pixels.

VICTOR. How very modern.

JESS. I'm the bleeding edge of culture, man. Except I want
to kill myself.

VICTOR. Oh please. Suicide is the most BANAL choice a
human can make.

JESS. Except when one's life is even more banal than the
choice to end it. Which in my opinion is less of a choice
and more of a way to quiet the noise.

VICTOR. Yikes.

JESS. My father died of self-inflicted wounds. Um. So. What
about you? What's your "deal?"

VICTOR. I'm all over the place. Right now I drive a gypsy
cab.

JESS. Are you a prostitute?

VICTOR. Should I take that as an insult or a compliment?

JESS. Or a trust-fundie?

VICTOR. *Now* I'm insulted.

JESS. Just trying to figure out how you got the cash for those sick duds.

VICTOR. I made these.

JESS. Made.

VICTOR. Sewed. Cut. Fitted. Et cetera.

JESS. Color me dazzled.

VICTOR. I have aspirations. Also it's difficult to find things in my size for grown-ups.

JESS. You don't eat I assume.

VICTOR. Food is for the weak and for women who hate themselves.

JESS. Here's to low self-esteem.

(They clink glasses and drink.)

VICTOR. Your ass is kind of huge.

JESS. Well.

VICTOR. It's like two trashbags filled with sadness

JESS. How could you be that drunk already?

VICTOR. I'm not. I'm just an asshole.

JESS. Good thing I dig assholes.

VICTOR. I guess you're the chick whose friends tell her she should date better dudes.

JESS. I don't have friends. And I don't date. I just fuck.

VICTOR. People don't "just fuck." That's a movie dream.

JESS. I do. I'm like your mom's worst nightmare. Self-employed self-destructive and omnivorous. Speaking of moms. Mine's dying.

VICTOR. I'm sorry.

JESS. I haven't talked to her in seven years. Her neighbor just sent me an email yesterday saying it's gotten serious. She thinks I should go out there.

(VICTOR takes a dramatic drag of his cigarette.)

VICTOR. Listening.

JESS. My mother is a smoker too. She buys Parliaments by the carton and lights up before her bowl of Special K every morning. She holds her cigarette high up in her knuckles and gestures casually it's like the cigarette is a sixth finger. She likes to guess how much weight I've gained just by looking at me. When I was growing up she filled my closet with beautiful, expensive clothes that were always a size too small, hoping I'd feel inspired to fit into them one day. I'm not sure why I'm still talking.

VICTOR. Because you need something ineffable and I'm standing right here?

JESS. Maybe. And maybe you're not even real. You're made of pixels. Or dust.

VICTOR. I don't know whether to hold you or to ask you to take me home.

JESS. Both. Please.

>   *(**VICTOR** holds **JESS**.)*

VICTOR. Take me home.

>   *(He does.)*

>   *(Lights up on **JESS** and **VICTOR** in bed together. **VICTOR** sleeps.)*

>   *(The **MODELS** are the bed. The walls. The take-out containers.)*

JESS. *(to us)* We lay in my queen bed for three straight days, stopping only to eat and watch DVDs and have sex on my tartan sheets. The salesgirl at Bed Bath & Beyond begged me not to buy them because they looked "mannish," so of course I had to.

Turns out he's a pretty selfish lover. It isn't epic at all. But at least it's real. More or less.

For breakfast we have museli and rice milk. For lunch we make pizza bagels in my toaster oven. And for dinner each of the three nights we order thai food. He of course eats nothing. But he smokes. A lot.

My phone rings constantly at first. It's my job. I only answer it once.

(She answers the phone.)

Hello?

LEWIS. *(on the phone)* They said the Saratoga – you know the Saratoga? The big war ship? They said the Saratoga is actually sailing today. Sort-of.

JESS. Get out.

LEWIS. Ya. It's being dragged by tugboats across the river so they can renovate it. It hasn't moved in twenty-four years. Did you know that thing survived five kamikaze suicide attacks in World War II? And a port attack in Vietnam.

JESS. Did you see that on the Who Gives a Shit network?

LEWIS. You sound better. Are you?

JESS. Nope. My ass is still two russet potatoes sitting in a scarf.

LEWIS. Don't *you* like to hyperbolize to make yourself seem compelling.

JESS. Don't *you* like to violate your therapist with a frozen turkey frank.

LEWIS. I told you that in confidence.

JESS. How are you?

LEWIS. Neutral. Although last night I made the grave tactical error of attending an after-work happy hour. Cara made a hostile play for me.

JESS. That girl drives me batty. Always wants to know what your "deal" is.

LEWIS. She was *relentless.* "Why haven't we hung out yet? Why don't you ever go for drinks with us?" Bwak bwak bwak. I was slowly inching away the entire time.

JESS. She's using you to score nerd cred. You'd better not make out with her.

LEWIS. I'd rather gag myself with an insulated chip insertion/extraction clipper. Oh Jesus. Kevin G. from MDP just IMed me. The secure server is not processing orders correctly. Something to do with variables.

JESS. Forward me what he sent you, then ask him to send the EXACT error message his customers are receiving –

LEWIS. Nope. You're going on a trip to visit your dying mother.

JESS. I'm not ready.

LEWIS. Do it.

JESS. No! I'm trying to preserve what little dignity I have.

LEWIS. It's a "cusp-of-mortality" visit. There a loophole in the dignity rulebook for that.

JESS. I need a more convincing argument, dude.

LEWIS. Um, how 'bout you don't need another massive regret careening you into another random penis?

JESS. Too late maybe?

LEWIS. Is he there right now?

JESS. Maybe?

LEWIS. What does he look like?

JESS. The usual. Emaciated. Caffeinated. Perforated with angst.

LEWIS. Don't let him stay more than four days. He'll sell your bike and leave pit stains in your T-shirts.

JESS. This one's different.

LEWIS. How so?

JESS. I'm not sure he actually exists.

LEWIS. I'm booking you a ticket. Little Rock, right?

JESS. No.

LEWIS. I'll tell Kevin you are having a family crisis.

JESS. I don't want to fly.

LEWIS. A rental then. We have a corporate account with Hertz.

JESS. Seriously, though, stop.

LEWIS. Death stops for no one, baby.

JESS. My credit cards are maxed.

LEWIS. This one's on me. Come back with just one tiny issue semi-resolved and I will feel somewhat validated as a human.

JESS. I don't exist to validate you.

LEWIS. Booking…

JESS. She can't see me like this! I'm a fucking slob –

LEWIS. Booked! Emailing confirmation now. Bring me back a souvenir from the Clinton library. Photocopy, bookmark, semen sample –

*(She hangs up. **VICTOR** awakens.)*

VICTOR. Your breasts are like little affable puppy heads. I just want to pet them.

JESS. Well your dick is like a failed hard drive.

VICTOR. What's a hard drive?

JESS. Tell me again how huge my ass is.

VICTOR. Your ass is so fucking huge it looks like you're shop-lifting throw pillows.

JESS. Weak!

VICTOR. It's 4 a.m. My "A" game is still hours away.

(He lights his last cigarette.)

Last smoke. Does this mean I have to actually leave the bed or do you think we can bribe the delivery guy to seize a pack?

JESS. Well considering I'm going to ask you to leave after you finish that cigarette, I'd say don't sweat it too much.

VICTOR. Was it something I said?

JESS. No. You're just a little too beautiful and I'm a little too fucked up.

VICTOR. I thought that was kind of working for us.

JESS. And, I need to leave town for a little while.

VICTOR. To where?

JESS. Gotta go see a man about a dog.

VICTOR. And that man is…boyfriend?

JESS. Nope.

VICTOR. Husband?

JESS. *Nein.*

VICTOR. Wife?

JESS. *Nyet.*

VICTOR. Mommy?

JESS. Stop that.

VICTOR. Ding-ding-ding!!

JESS. I don't like being *sussed.*

VICTOR. Tell me a story. From your childhood.

JESS. And, I don't like talking about myself.

VICTOR. Okay, tell yourself one. Act like I'm not here.

JESS. Fine. What about?

VICTOR. Um. Cigarettes. You got any smoking stories?

>   *(beat)*

JESS. Why would I? Wait actually, yes. I do have a smoking story.

VICTOR. Rockin'. Carry on.

JESS. Shit. Um okay so I'm eleven years old, and I'm *very* odd. I play D&D by myself. I hoard Mars bars. I have no friends. I am the polar opposite of my mother at that age. She has no idea what to do with me. So she decides to "make an effort." She takes us on the only mother/daughter vacation we'll ever have.

VICTOR. Where'd you go?

JESS. A motel a few miles from where we lived.

VICTOR. That's so sad. Wah.

JESS. She gets us two adjoining rooms for a week and closes her door. I don't see her for days. On the fourth day I see this girl standing by the Pepsi machine. Skinny as a corpse, face full of freckles –

VICTOR. So this is the '80s, right?

JESS. Yeah.

VICTOR. What is she wearing?

JESS. Pegged Jordaches. Checkerboard Keds.

VICTOR. Jesus Christ I want to SEX the '80s. Continue.

JESS. So she looks me up and down and asks me if there's anything fun to do around here. I'm like, "smoke."

VICTOR. You smoked at eleven? Tsk tsk.

JESS. No! I'm gonna fake it. I swipe a pack of Parliaments off my mother's dresser. Find Freckles by the soda machine. She suggests we hide out in the maintenance closet.

VICTOR. Dirtbag.

JESS. So there we are. In the closet. She lights my cigarette and I inhale. I know I'm not doing it right, but I cannot bring myself to imitate my mother. I take shallow, timid puffs from the tips of my fingers.

But this girl's the real deal…a scarf of air and ash curling around her head…

I think I realize in that moment I will never be something worth looking at. Like my mother was. I'll always be the one looking.

So she peers at me strangely, with like a touch of like, malice. And suddenly, the lights are out. A hand is touching my breast. I forgot to wear my training bra. I can't move, can't breathe. Then the lights flick on again. And she's laughing at me.

She drops her cigarette. Says, "Thanks for the smoke." And leaves.

I want to tell my mother. I run back to her room. Knock. No answer. Try the knob. Locked. Open the door of our adjoining bathroom. She's at her open window… – and I say, "momma." Nothing for like three full minutes. Then she says…

MODELS. He loved the wrong one.

JESS. Just like that.

VICTOR. Was she drunk?

JESS. Sleepwalking. I touch her arm and she wakes up and says…

MODELS. Why am I here?

JESS. And then…

MODELS. What's the matter, love? You look so sad.

JESS. And then.

MODELS. You're breaking out. You need to wash your face every night. Don't ruin your complexion, Jessica. You'll have no future if you don't take care of yourself now.

JESS. And then.

MODELS. I love you. You know that.

> *(longish beat)*

VICTOR. Your exit from childhood was through the butt end of cigarette.

JESS. Suppose it was.

VICTOR. I am so happy to know that. Guess what? I have something to show you.

> *(VICTOR blows his last breath of smoke from his mouth. It curls around his head like a beautiful ash scarf.)*

> *(Then… The parade of MODELS wearing wispy grey dresses and gowns struts through the room. They are dressed as though they are wearing a gown of smoke.)*

JESS. You made that for me?

VICTOR. Indeed.

JESS. Wait. You can see them!

VICTOR. Of course.

JESS. How?

VICTOR. Because I'm fucking made of light.

> *(They watch the fashion show for a while. Music, etc. Then, the MODELS disappear.)*

JESS. Wanna take a trip to the South?

> *(Freeze on them.)*

> *(Lights up on ESME in the workroom in the '70s, sketching. She wears something amazing, as usual.)*

(**LOUELLA**, *a cheerful ruddy woman wearing horrible clothes, pops her head in.*)

LOUELLA. Hi!

I'm here!

Sorry I'm so late

I had to take a cab

The subways are so confusing!

I'm staying at the Best Western.

Louella Wilkens?

I won tickets on KCFW?

Um in Little Rock Arkansas?

VIP fashion treatment?

All-inclusive package?

Two nights in a three star hotel?

Tour of the studio?

Headband?

(silence)

I was trying to win Simon and Garfunkel tickets

I asked around about you folks afterwards

The name rang a bell

A little bell

I don't really follow fashion

I just go to Dillards and buy what's on the sale rack

Is someone boiling an egg?

ESME. *(with contempt)* Is that what you're wearing right now?

Dillards?

LOUELLA. I don't think that's the brand

It's just where I got it.

I mean it's comfortable and doesn't make my ass look huge.

I also like a little give in the waist

Oh and I hate itchy fabrics

And stuff I have to dry clean.

Such a hassle.

(More silence. She retrieves a Tupperware from her bag.)

LOUELLA. I made these. They're cupcakes. Brought them on the plane.

I got creative with the frosting.

I like to be creative. I paint.

Watercolors. Landscapes.

Last spring I had a little showing in our community room

Neighbors mostly

Some girls from my office

And guess what!

I sold two paintings!

And a rocking chair.

Someone right now is rocking in front of my artwork

Drinking a lemonade and feeling good about life.

> *(beat)*

I cannot stop talking.

> *(She tries to hand* **ESME** *the Tupperware.* **ESME** *does not take them.)*

Just cupcakes. They don't bite.

ESME. I don't imbibe sugar.

LOUELLA. Well no wonder you're so skinny!

Like everyone else in this city

I've never seen such skinny people

Except my cousin with MS

And you're so pretty

Are you Mr. Cavanaugh's assistant?

ESME. No.

LOUELLA. Oh. Are you a model?

ESME. Former.

LOUELLA. How glamorous! What do you do now?

ESME. I'm Victor's muse.

LOUELLA. Muse! Sounds like an important job.

Is he around?

ESME. Not yet.

LOUELLA. I don't often get to see famous people in person.

Once? When I was a waitress at our local greasy spoon?

Smokey Robinson came in to eat one night

I served him coffee and toast

and afterwards they had to tell me he was someone special!

You know what I said?

"Everyone is someone special."

The more people who *see* how special you are

The more famous you become –

ESME. Oh my god you really need to shut the fuck up.

I mean Jesus. I know New York City is a VERY exciting place but could you at least try to keep your shit together?

> *(beat)*

LOUELLA. You might be a little cranky from the not-eating?

You know a cupcake would solve a lot of your problems.

> **(VICTOR** *walks in, fraught, and a little exhilarated.)*

VICTOR. I couldn't sleep Esme. All night, in my head. Piper dangling from a lighting fixture in her mother's kitchen. I've crossed over into something. I'm afraid of myself.

> *(beat)*

LOUELLA. Fashion designer.

VICTOR. Louella Wilkens. A pleasure. Welcome to the East Village! Bet you had to step over a few bodies on the way in. Don't worry, they're not dead. Just coming off the heroin. Don't take pictures of them or they'll hunt you down and slip their pinkies in your butthole. Ha ha ha ha!! Gumball?

LOUELLA. Please.

(She takes a gumball from the machine.)

VICTOR. I see you've met the incomparable Esme Varick. Esme is the soul of the Victor Cavanaugh line. Before she came along I was making clothes for myself alone and costumes for the occasional broke theatre troupe –

ESME. I'm going outside to smoke.

(She exits.)

VICTOR. Without that woman, I'm just a hand sewing the air without any thread.

LOUELLA. I was having trouble looking at her directly
Like staring into the sun

VICTOR. Yes, she's always been like that. Sort of brutally beautiful. Like an alien.

LOUELLA. Where'd you find her?

VICTOR. Sipping coffee on the Bowery one summer afternoon. Wearing this magnificent outlandish Betsy Johnson cocktail dress – miles and miles of pink taffeta and a huge red sash with a bow on the back. Absurd. She wore drama like it was skin.

(Outside, ESME *smokes, and remembers.)*

ESME. I was so hung over from a party the night before… hadn't even changed my clothes…

VICTOR. I begged her to come back to my studio and try on these tuxedo pants I had just sewn for myself…

ESME. I told him yes, on the condition he let me pass out in his bed for a few hours…

VICTOR. I brought her back to my tiny apartment in Chinatown. Fabrics, patterns everywhere. A sty. She unzipped her dress, draped it over a chair, and passed out in my bed…

ESME. …and when I woke up, a square of sunlight from his tiny window perfectly framed his outrageous purple and grey Spectators. "A stunning shoe," I thought. And he emerged from the bathroom, damp and fruity and bearded. And moments later I smelled bacon and coffee, and I met him by his ancient stove where he stood cooking me dinner.

I left a piece of myself in that kitchen that day.

VICTOR. By fall she was walking in my menswear line.

LOUELLA. Must be hard to have everyone staring all the time.

Oh who am I kidding, I would love that

VICTOR. The attention?

LOUELLA. Everything

The glamour

The fuss

Never having to worry about your greasy hair or your lady paunch

Ah well you know

I realized pretty young I'd never be something worth looking at.

That I'd always be the one looking

But I suppose there's some grace in that too...

(small beat)

VICTOR. Do you mind me asking a personal question?

LOUELLA. I'm not married.

I live next door to my mother.

She's a firecracker

We have a good time.

VICTOR. I was going to ask how much you pay for your clothes.

LOUELLA. Oh.

Everyone likes a good deal

But I suppose I would pay for quality

I'm at that point in my life

I've bought cheaply made clothes before

They just don't last!

I'd rather spend fifty dollars on a good pair of shoes

That I can wear for years

Than five dollars on a pair that falls apart in a month.
I work too hard to waste my money on trash.

VICTOR. What else do you like?

Fashion-wise.

LOUELLA. Gosh, um…

Bright colors?
But not too bright?
I love honey butter
Such a pretty name
I tend to like things that are food-colored
Coffee, toffee, cherry, rum, eggplant, mint
Oh! Here. I made these. Back home.

(She hands him a Tupperware container.)

They're cupcakes.

I got creative and made designs on them.

*(**VICTOR** stands slowly and approaches **LOUELLA.**)*

(He takes a cupcake and examines it.)

VICTOR. Is this a cubist painting?

LOUELLA. I don't know what it is.

*(He peels it slowly. He eats it very slowly. **LOUELLA** watches him. It seems to go on forever. He finishes the cupcake.)*

VICTOR. That was.

Perfectly.

Average.

PART TWO

Longing

(Lights on **JESS** *and* **VICTOR** *waiting at Hertz,
present day. They sit on a step.* **JESS** *watches*
VICTOR *as he sketches into a pad.* **JESS** *eats a
bagel.* **VICTOR** *again wears a stunning ensemble.)*

(The **MODELS** *are objects, again.)*

JESS. We're at a car lot in Brooklyn waiting for our rental.
I left all my flannels at home
'Cause if I showed up in cotton plaid
She would eat me alive

So
As he draws
I munch on a terrible bagel –

VICTOR. Who are you talking to?

JESS. It's my inner monologue. Who asked you to listen?

VICTOR. You're sitting right next to me. It's fucking
annoying. Talk to me if you want to talk.

JESS. I – wow, okay. Look at that girl.

(A **MODEL** *walks by with black spikey hair and
a bike chain around her neck. Pauses, lights a
cigarette.)*

VICTOR. Probably on her way to Coney Island to buy
heroin.

JESS. I wanna be her.

VICTOR. Why on earth?

JESS. She's impenetrable. Like a fortress.
I could be her.

VICTOR. No you couldn't.

JESS. Why not?

VICTOR. You're "Flannel Bagel Girl."

JESS. I'm not fucking Flannel Bagel Girl!

> (**JESS** *approaches a gumball machine, which is a* **MODEL.** *Grabs a gumball. Eyes the bike chain girl.*)

VICTOR. Sugar...

JESS. I think better when I'm chewing. Should I get a leather jacket?

VICTOR. Absolutely not.

JESS. Or a bunch of safety pins?

VICTOR. She isn't real anyway. She's a projection of your desire to feel less vulnerable.

> (**VICTOR** *waves her away. She vanishes.*)

JESS. Right.

Ever get scared the only thing you might be good at is longing?

VICTOR. Nope. If I *did* though, I would try to sell it. On a street corner in Queens. Under the 7 train. Mason jars filled with pale yellow cotton I soaked overnight.

JESS. How mercenary.

VICTOR. Buying shit makes people feel powerful and sexy. And creating the shit people want to buy makes *us* immortal. I was born to be a God.

JESS. Is that why you're so rotten in bed?

VICTOR. Um, no. I'm rotten in bed because I'm a narcissist and I don't like losing control.

You haven't told me you love my outfit yet.

JESS. I love your outfit. I really do.

VICTOR. The fabric is from Guatemala. I spent some time there after I lost my mind. Most people would never think of combining brocade and stripes. And I've made the perfect flare for my legs. You wanna live inside that flare, admit it.

JESS. I do...

VICTOR. Chew yourself a little nest of thread and lint, and curl up into that massive hem –

JESS. When did you lose your mind?

VICTOR. After my sister died.

JESS. How did she die?

VICTOR. It's not something I talk about.

JESS. Try.

> *(beat)*

VICTOR. She um. Withered away in childhood sickness. Went from apple-cheeked to gaunt and brittle in a matter of weeks. It was horrible. We were…close…

> *(Beat. He's having trouble. Deep breath.)*

So.

I left.

Poof.

Next flight to Central America.

Hopped from one diseased village to another

Surrounded myself with people who confront crippling loss on a daily basis

So I could learn how to cope.

JESS. Did you?

VICTOR. No.

But I *did* learn what I needed to do with my life.

JESS. Become a God?

VICTOR. Re-write the dying process.

Take things that've been ravaged

And make them *ravishing*

JESS. Oh.

Gosh.

Is that what I'm supposed to do?

VICTOR. Listen, Bagel

Take the things that damage you.

And then…

Own them.

JESS. But *how?*

> (**VICTOR** *becomes deliberately distracted by his outfit.*)

VICTOR. I'm not the best vehicle for my clothes…

JESS. Come on…

VICTOR. My physique lacks drama –

JESS. Please…

VICTOR. It's like I'm faking it –

JESS. Tell me how to be…

VICTOR. But we're all faking it, I guess.

> (*Beat, pointed.*)

Aren't we.

JESS. *(to us)* At that moment, our car pulls up. And we get in. And we drive. I eat turkey jerky in the front seat while he sews clothes in the back. And then, night happens.

> (*Night happens. They freeze.*)

> (*Lights up on* **VICTOR***'s studio in the '70s. Music plays.** **LOUELLA** *stands on a small step, wearing a close-fitting neutral garment.*)

> (**VICTOR** *retrieves a tape measure from a box of supplies and approaches her.*)

> (*Somewhere else,* **ESME** *cuts fabric, sketches, dyes, etc.*)

VICTOR. Simplicity. Not something I'm drawn to normally.

LOUELLA. Well there's so much noise already in the world am I right?

> (**VICTOR** *lays the tape on* **LOUELLA***'s left wrist and gently measures from wrist to shoulder.* **ESME** *rips fabric.*)

---

*Please see Music Use Note on page 3

VICTOR. I don't understand it honestly. I mean I get utility, I dig that. But if you could choose between something that defines your identity with a glance and something that erases you completely, why would you choose to be erased?

> *(**VICTOR** removes the tape from **LOUELLA***'s arm and wraps it around her waist. She holds her breath. **ESME** dyes cloth.)*

LOUELLA. Well…

You grow up with a set of…values

And it takes effort to…

to make yourself into something outside your up-bringing

So…why would you?

Especially if you have no reason to?

> *(**LOUELLA** exhales. **VICTOR** slowly wraps the tape measure around **LOUELLA***'s hips. **ESME** sketches noisily.)*

VICTOR. But I feel like that's a natural part of becoming a cognizant, curious adult. You shuffle off the dead skin of your upbringing and open up a dialogue with society by outfitting yourself in a way that speaks to your vision of your innermost self.

> *(**VICTOR** gently lifts **LOUELLA***'s arms, then slowly, very slowly, wraps the tape measure around her chest. **ESME** cuts paper aggressively.)*

> *(We see **LOUELLA** uwaken to him…)*

LOUELLA. But what if that "vision"

is the same as those around you?

What if you *want* to be like

The people who defined you?

VICTOR. I guess this is where I get lost.

> *(**VICTOR** slowly wraps the tape measure around **LOUELLA***'s neck. His lips are very close to her ear as she talks. **ESME** pastes fabric swaths onto paper.)*

LOUELLA. I don't think it's "banal"

to celebrate the things about one's community and lifestyle

that one finds comforting.

VICTOR. Do you think others feel the same as you?

LOUELLA. I think so.

At least everyone I know does.

The girls I work with

My mom

> *(beat)*

> (**VICTOR** *lowers himself to his knees in front of* **LOUELLA**. *He places the tape measure at her ankle, then tracks it upwards to her inner thigh.* **ESME** *throws glitter at her work.*)

VICTOR. Must be nice to have things so uncomplicated.

LOUELLA. Sometimes when I listen to you

I feel like you must have suffered a lot

VICTOR. How can you tell that?

LOUELLA. Just a sense I get

Like I can see inside your soul

You have a storm in you

> *(small beat)*

VICTOR. It's not something I talk about.

LOUELLA. Not even to Esme?

> (**ESME** *stops breathing.*)

> (**VICTOR** *begins to stroke* **LOUELLA**'*s inner thigh very lightly.*)

VICTOR. Especially not her. She thinks I'm a… She has expectations of me. It's flattering. I mean, sometimes. Part of me wants to be the man she sees. Very badly. But another part, perhaps a larger part, wants to… to sleep. For a very long time. And wake up wanting different things. And be okay with that.

LOUELLA. Two months ago I wanted to win my office pool
A month's supply of Campbell's soup, assorted flavors.

VICTOR. And now?

> *(**LOUELLA** gently guides **VICTOR**'s hand to the zipper on her pants.)*

LOUELLA. I want to be beautiful.

> *(**VICTOR** begins to undress her. They freeze. As does **ESME**.)*

> *(Lights up on **JESS** and **VICTOR** in the car. **JESS** drives while **VICTOR** sleeps in the back seat. He is surrounded by fabric. **JESS** gnaws on some turkey jerky and talks to him quietly while he sleeps.)*

> *(The **MODELS** are the car.)*

JESS. I am stroking the space between your ear and your shoulder
I am stroking the space between your hip and your thigh
I am stroking the space between your / spine and

VICTOR. Shut up please

JESS. Sorry.

> *(He goes back to sleep. **JESS** drives. She drives some more. Suddenly, she notices a sign on the road.)*

480 miles to Little Rock.
Halfway there.

> *(Panic washes over her.)*

You know what I think about? All the time?
The distance between a person's nature and her desire to be loved.

VICTOR. Your nature and your desire to be loved are the same fucking thing

JESS. No, my nature is to run the hell away from anything that even resembles love. And I have no idea how to close the gap!

VICTOR. Don't you think you should figure that out before
we get to Little Rock?

JESS. I'm trying!

I mean, I'd have to become an entirely different person

Shuffle off the dead skin of my upbringing

Murder my child self

Just suicide the shit outa her

VICTOR. And then what?

JESS. I wish I knew.

> *(She drives some more.)*

VICTOR. Pull over.

JESS. What?

VICTOR. Now!

> *(He grabs the wheel and pulls over violently…)*

JESS. What the fuck!

VICTOR. What are you doing?

JESS. Driving! That is so dangerous, what you just did.

VICTOR. I mean, what are you doing with your PERSON.

JESS. You mean my what. My being, my soul…?

VICTOR. All of it.

JESS. I haven't thought that far!

VICTOR. Think it.

What happens after *right now.*

JESS. I…gosh… I guess we'll stop at KFC and get a double
down with a side of potato wedges, then get a motel
for the night, and then drive some more, then another
motel, and then maybe a quickie trip to Dillards and
get a sweater or whatever, something that doesn't make
me look like a total pig, and eventually I'll like, I'll
show up at her bedside and she'll be looking at me
with those perpetually bewildered eyes, marveling yet
again at how two stunning individuals could have made
such a non-person…

VICTOR. And then what?

JESS. I don't know…

VICTOR. Back to New York? Back to your bagels and your burritos and your blotchiness?

JESS. I don't know, ok?

>   *(beat)*

VICTOR. How old were you when you left Little Rock?

JESS. Eighteen.

VICTOR. So your mother literally has not seen you in over a decade.

JESS. No.

VICTOR. So she has no idea what you look like anymore.

JESS. No.

VICTOR. Good.
Who would you like to be by the end of this car ride?

JESS. Um.
Future Jess?

VICTOR. And who is she?

JESS. She's much thinner than me.

VICTOR. Of course.

JESS. Her hair isn't greasy.

VICTOR. Never.

JESS. She doesn't pop her zits. She buys expensive creams for her face, like Clinique and Kiehls.

VICTOR. More.

JESS. She goes to yoga five mornings a week. She skips breakfast when she isn't hungry. She cleans her bathroom regularly. Waxes her vag. Gets facials.

VICTOR. Well maintained.

JESS. She knows her inseam. When Future Jess dines out, she orders her wine by the region. She, um.

VICTOR. *More.*

JESS. She gets blow outs. She doesn't give blow jobs to randoms. Future Jess has awesome posture. She never goes to bars alone. She doesn't get steak and eggs delivered to her at 3 a.m. from her local diner. Oh, AND. Open-toed shoes DO NOT embarrass her.

VICTOR. My my. Future Jess is so *bougie.*

JESS. She's not for you. She's for my fucking mother.

VICTOR. Sounds like we need to hatch her.

JESS. We do.

VICTOR. It'll probably hurt.

JESS. I know.

>   *(beat)*

VICTOR. Okay

JESS. Right now?

>   (**VICTOR** *nods.* **JESS** *gets out of the car.*)

VICTOR. Do you know who you're saying goodbye to?

JESS. A flawed person.

An ordinary person.

VICTOR. And do you know why?

JESS. To make myself into someone worth looking at.

VICTOR. And how badly do you want to eviscerate yourself?

JESS. Pretty fucking bad, dude.

VICTOR. Okay. Prepare thyself.

>   (**JESS** *crunches down, cringing.*)

JESS. Go!

VICTOR. *(vicious)* Your ass.

It is so fat that when you sit down you're a foot taller.

When you go to the airport you get arrested for ten pounds of crack.

Your ass beeps when you walk backwards.

Your ass is so big, I need a sherpa to guide me around it.

It looks like two pigs fighting over a milk dud.

Like a double-stuffed oreo without the cookies

From behind you look like Orson Wells in a tank top.

You should go to the emergency room for cardiac ASS-rest.

It looks like you're smuggling a family of gypsies

It's like two bacon basketballs shitting under a polyester
tent

Hey fatass! King Kong wants his nutsack back!

> *(Suddenly, out of nowhere, the pack of* **MODELS**
> *from* **VICTOR***'s first fashion show stampede in
> wearing their spiked heels and animal prints.
> They charge* **JESS** *and mow her down, screeching
> and roaring like a wild pack of animals.* **JESS**
> *disappears in the frenzy. It's pretty violent.)*

> *(Then…they pass.* **JESS** *emerges wearing a chic
> leopard coat and some open-toed shoes. She is
> scraped up and bruised, bleeding. But fashionable.)*

Nosebleed chic. Entry-level. Didn't have a lot to work
with but it'll do.

JESS. Um… I'm…

VICTOR. You okay?

JESS. I'm not sure who I am.

VICTOR. You are who I want you to be. Isn't that why I'm
here?

> *(Beat.* **JESS** *steps out of time for a second.)*

JESS.

THIS IS THE SONG THAT HAPPENS
WHEN I RUN OUT OF WORDS

HMMMMM-MMMMMM-MMMMMM
I SING ABOUT MY FEARS
THEY ARE ORDINARY FEARS

HMMMMM-MMMMMM-MMMMMM

THEY ARE FEARS ABOUT BECOMING
THE RUG BENEATH YOUR FEET
THE HAIR INSIDE YOUR BRUSH
THE HOOK FOR YOUR UMBRELLA
THE INK WITHIN YOUR PEN
EVERYTHING YOU TOUCH
BUT NOTHING YOU NOTICE

HMMMMM-MMMMMM-MMMMMM

EVERYTHING YOU TOUCH
BUT NOTHING YOU NOTICE

HMMMMM-MMMMMM-MMMMMM
HMMMMM-MMMMMM-MMMMMM
HMMMMM

> (**JESS** *steps back into time.* **VICTOR** *is waiting.*)

> *(beat)*

Okay.

> *(Freeze on them. Lights fade.)*

End of Act One

Act Two

*(Lights up on the workroom in the '70s. Scraps in
butter, toffee, coffee, cherry, rum, eggplant, and
mint cover the ground.)*

*(Roxy Music's "Love Is the Drug" plays incredibly
loudly.*)*

*(ESME stands in the center of the room on a block
as VICTOR drapes fabric on her. They shout over
the music.)*

ESME. I hate these fucking colors! They look like what
you'd paint a dentist's office to distract from the pain! I
hope you're using them ironically!

VICTOR. You gained weight, Esme!

ESME. I ate a grape yesterday, sue me. Listen. I was up all
night thinking about G.I. Jezebel! I'm in LOVE. Here's
what we do: Turn down the aggression and pump up
the mutant! GO DISCO!

VICTOR. What?

ESME. The club dancing? With the mirror balls and the
platform shoes?

VICTOR. Why don't I know about this?

ESME. Because it exists outside of your head! A lot of things
do!

VICTOR. Listen, I need to tell you something!

ESME. I hate it!

VICTOR. Hate what!

ESME. Whatever you're about to tell me!

(VICTOR turns the record player down.)

*Please see Music Use Note on page 3

VICTOR. I've invited Louella Wilkens to help consult for my fall line.

ESME. Sorry, who?

VICTOR. You know exactly who.

ESME. Are you fucking serious?

VICTOR. As death.

ESME. Christ, Victor. Why don't you just take a shame-walk through the Misses department at Sears? There are simpler ways to corrupt yourself.

VICTOR. I'm not looking to be corrupted. I'm looking to be influenced. I am completely out of touch with ninety-nine point nine percent of this country. I never leave this store, I never turn on the TV. I barely read the trades. Did you know Monday in Blue just filed for bankruptcy?

ESME. Serves them right for ripping you off every season.

VICTOR. And Pasha is going under too. If I don't employ corrective measures... I mean I'm a terrible businessman, I don't know what else to do. If I wind up driving that fucking gypsy cab around Chinatown again –

ESME. Maybe it's time to grab your scissors and crawl way way back into that tiny dark corner of your brain and start stabbing.

(*Beat.* **VICTOR** *realizes she's making fun of him.*)

VICTOR. You think you know me, Esme. You think you know me but there are some things –

ESME. Yes you're very tormented Victor. I get it. And truthfully, I don't want to know everything about you.

VICTOR. Because you believe you already do.

ESME. *Point being,* your impulses are yours. And... I want to help you protect them. Because I have unlimited faith in you. So. Okay fine. If you need to, um roll that barrel of turkey grease out from Fucksville USA and gawk at her for a few weeks so you can get the tickle back in your nutsack, I'm here for you.

VICTOR. I've invited her to stay with me.

>   *(beat)*

ESME. In your. In your *apartment?*

VICTOR. I'm flying her out. I don't have the money to put her up as well.

ESME. She can't put herself up?

VICTOR. She's using her vacation time for this. I need to play this out, Esme.

ESME. Great. Anything I can do to help just let me know.

VICTOR. You could pick her up at the airport.

>   *(beat)*

ESME. Sure.

>   *(Freeze on them.)*

>   *(Lights up on the motel room, present day.* **VICTOR** *sits on the bed, smoking. A fabric frenzy has erupted in the room.)*

VICTOR. Ready?

JESS. *(from off)* Do it!

>   *(***VICTOR*** *plays "Fame" by David Bowie* from his record player. [or some better, less-well-known '70s song].)*

>   *(***JESS*** *prances in wearing high heels, a feathered wig, and her underwear. She's still a little beat up, and uncertain.)*

>   *(The* **MODELS** *are the motel room.)*

VICTOR. *(shouting with tyrannical glee)* Hairline lucite, diaphanous
Winged brows the color of anthracite
flying-nun-meets-flying-saucer!

>   *(***JESS*** *teases out her wig.)*

Eyes, lips: trash-bag black

---

*Please see Music Use Note on page 3

(JESS *applies dark eye makeup to her eyes, then mascara.*)

VICTOR. No lashes! Get rid of the lashes!

(*She sits to wipe off the mascara.*)

Don't sit down!!!!

(*She stands.*)

Drape! Cover!

(*She grabs several layers of fabric from the floor, draping herself in them. She then grabs her coat and tosses it over her shoulders. She smolders throughout.*)

Feel the swing-weight of that coat?
Let it walk you like a wolf
Kinetic dimentia!

(JESS *walks like a wolf on her hind legs, howling.*)

Back with hips, forward with face
MORE FACE!

(JESS *gives more face.*)

A smile like burning tar

(JESS *gives off a smell like burning tar.*)

Smile, not smell!

(JESS *corrects.*)

Feathers. Human hair. Spoilt milk.

(JESS *is confused.*)

JESS. Spoilt...?

VICTOR. I don't know what it means
But YOU MUST.

(JESS *does a soft-shoe in her high heels.*)

I want to hear those heels
Make them talk
Make them tell me I have NO SOUL

*(*JESS *whips her shoes off her feet, tucks her fists inside, and manipulates them like puppets.)*

JESS. *(puppet voice)* You have no soul!

*(*VICTOR *turns off the music.* JESS *grabs a bag of candy.)*

VICTOR. So much better.

JESS. *(not really)* Right? I felt it this time!

VICTOR. We just need to work on your power. It's all attitude, Future Jess. Believe you are the most cunning, rare creature on the planet and that if anyone dares look away his eyeballs will shrivel into tiny smoldering raisins in his head. Also –

(He grabs the bag of candy from her.)

You need to stop fooding. NOW.

JESS. Those had peanuts –

VICTOR. Just stop.

JESS. What if she can tell I'm faking it?

VICTOR. You won't be faking anything. This is Future Jess. She never met Future Jess. Future Jess was born on the side of the road in West Virgina three days ago.

JESS. Paint my toenails.

*(*JESS *flops on the bed hands the bottle of nail polish to* VICTOR. *He begins painting her toenails.)*

(to us) We're at a motel in Memphis. Just two hours away from my mother's apartment. I haven't checked my email once. For all I know she's already dead. I search my body for an emotion regarding this, any at all. Nothing yet.

VICTOR. *(to us)* I pretend to have an inner monologue too, just so I can connect to myself in that introspective kind of way. But I'm absolutely not prone to introspection, so it's a complete failure.

JESS. I love my new clothes. They're perfect. I never buy expensive clothes for myself. But why would I? I loathe myself.

(**VICTOR** *lights up a cigarette.*)

VICTOR. Not anymore. Future Jess wants people to look at her...like...

> (*The clothing rises from the ground, and a model materializes inside it. The material becomes a beautiful architectural and flowing gown. It's trashy in its own way – partially ruined, but it is a foxy tragedy.*)

...her.

> (*The* **MODEL** *struts back and forth, as though the hotel room is a runway.*)

I made that for your mother.

JESS. It was her favorite. Page twenty-six of your Fall '71 Lookbook. She used to talk about the moment you conceived it. You were at a cafe in the East Village and you told a joke about sodomy and she laughed really hard and spilled mimosa all over herself...and you said you wanted to make a dress that looked like autumn and spilled mimosa and butt-sex and her laughter –

VICTOR. She'd wear it around my tiny apartment. Walk back and forth in her bare feet for hours. I'm watching the fabric move. Magnificent. I'm watching her frame compete with the frame of the whalebone. Her posture has to be straight as a blade or she'll get speared in the ribs. But I don't give a fuck what she thinks of it. Or what you think of it.

JESS. You couldn't have made it a little roomier?

VICTOR. No. She must be rail thin for it to work.

JESS. Why?

VICTOR. If she had killer cans or a big dumpy bottom, would you be interested in the clothes at all? Fashion is about self-denial and sacrifice. One must let oneself wither. Give into the death instinct.

> (*beat*)

JESS. You must have hated her.

VICTOR. Who?

JESS. My mother.

VICTOR. This is a loving homage –

JESS. She had to STARVE herself to fit into it! And it HURT her! How is that anything but sadistic?

VICTOR. There is beauty in the decimation, Jess. Your mother of all people knew that. And don't call me sadistic. It hurts my feelings.

JESS. You just said you don't care what I think.

VICTOR. I lied. It's my defense mechanism. I care very much what you think. And I'm ashamed about it.

JESS. If you're ashamed you can change it.

VICTOR. No. I can't. It's my tragic flaw.

JESS. Because you're a narcissist?

VICTOR. Bingo.

JESS. *(giddy)* You're the first one I've ever had.

VICTOR. You don't really have me, Jess. But you know that.

JESS. Don't say that –

> *(The motel phone rings. And rings… She stares at it.* **JESS** *answers.)*

Hello.

LEWIS. Your phone is totally off, dude.

JESS. How did you find me?

LEWIS. I'm a level twelve digital hunstman. I can stalk like a Navy Seal. What's with the radio silence?

JESS. I'm trying not to check messages.

LEWIS. Is *he* still with you?

JESS. Yep.

LEWIS. Leech, drunk, or perv?

JESS. Companion. And perv. He's an artist.

LEWIS. I'll bet you're painting his toenails right now.

JESS. Actually, he's painting mine.

LEWIS. *What?* WHO ARE YOU?

JESS. What do you mean?

LEWIS. Oh no. Are you wearing make-up?

JESS. So the fuck what?

LEWIS. What has he done to you?

JESS. Nothing. It's my choice.

LEWIS. You're going Gwyneth!

JESS. I am not going Gwyneth!

LEWIS. Ok. What did you have for lunch today?

JESS. Goodbye, Lewis.

LEWIS. Wait! Last night on the *30 Rock* marathon? Liz Lemon had a dentist appointment –

> (**JESS** *hangs up the phone.*)

VICTOR. That guy's in love with you –

JESS. I never want to talk to or about anyone ever again. No one exists but you. Okay? I want you to string a big net around us, a sticky gauzy gossamer cocoon made of like, tulle and hemp and body fluids, and no one will get in ever. Not with lasers. Not with machetes. Not with heartache or death or buzzwords or country songs. It's impermeable. Nothing but the sound of our own voices twining in and out of one another's ears. And our breathing.

VICTOR. Death will get in, though.

JESS. I know. But pretend it won't.

VICTOR. It will.

JESS. Pretend.

VICTOR. No

JESS. You have to.

VICTOR. I won't, Jess.

> *(beat)*

> *(The **MODEL** is still walking back and forth, as though on an endless runway.)*

> *(**VICTOR** and **JESS** watch her.)*

(Lights up on **VICTOR**'s *apartment.* **ESME** *enters in her sunglasses and awesome attire and goes to the burner as* **LOUELLA** *struggles with her massive suitcase.)*

LOUELLA. Well I am just a wilted flower

All that sitting! On the plane, then the car

We don't have traffic like that back home

Unless there's a horrible accident

My ears are still ringing from the radio

I hope you don't normally listen to it that loud

It isn't good for your –

ESME. Fuck you, Louella

You half-sack of un-kneaded dough

You half-eaten jelly donut

You probably voted for Nixon you bag of trash

Jamming your meaty hands into your polyester gut pocket

Shooting watercolors from your beefy horrible cunt

Washing your hair in the vomit from the farm animals you fuck

Even they hate you

You needy slut

You rocking chair cupcake shithead

You ruin him I will kill you

I will pluck out your beady little eyeballs

Fry them in olive oil

And feed them to the alley rats

> *(***ESME** *lights her cigarette on the burner and hands* **LOUELLA** *a set of keys.)*

Here's a set of keys. He doesn't keep food in the fridge because he doesn't eat, so shit out of luck there. Burners work but the oven's broken. He stores his cigarette cartons in there. Don't touch his fabrics, don't touch his sketches, don't move his soaps in the bathroom, he's weirdly anal about that. Don't drink that whiskey, it was a gift from a famous designer. Don't clean. He's weird about that. Don't answer the phone. The trumpet in the closet was his sister's who died of leukemia so don't touch that. The TV doesn't work, and neither does the toaster. Don't wash that wine stain off the counter. Don't lay a finger on any garment on any surface or hanger. The toilet has low water pressure and the shower only ever gets lukewarm. He has an air mattress for you but it leaks so you can sleep in his bed. For now.

> (**ESME** *pauses.*)

He, he has no extra bed linens so if you can't stand the smell of months-old man-body take them to the laundromat at the corner.

LOUELLA. Don't be upset because I'm the new muse. There's room for both of us.

But I'm not going back to Little Rock. Ever.

ESME. You aren't going to be famous, Louella. I hope you understand that.

> (*small beat*)

LOUELLA. I'll be whatever he makes me.

Maybe you can give me some tips.

> (*beat*)

> (**ESME** *reaches into her pocket and pulls out a bright red lipstick. She writes the letters "E-S-M-E" on the wall.*)

ESME. In case you need to spell it.

> (*She exits.* **LOUELLA** *sits down, takes in the room, takes a deep breath.*)

> (*Lights back up present day.* **VICTOR** *is nowhere to be found.*)

JESS. *(to us)* He's asleep inside. I'm outside panicking. And trying to smoke.

(All the MODELS parade before JESS, who is awake, panicked, trying to smoke. They wear the beautiful architectural trashy foxy gown.)

(to us, re: the MODELS.)

They won't go away. And Lewis keeps leaving messages.

(LEWIS appears, separately, in his own light.)

LEWIS. What-up, skank. I know you aren't checking messages but I figured I'd leave one for you anyway because I'm really really bored. So, an update. Work sucks. I went to Chipotle's today. Ordered a burrito bowl. They gave me a choice of black or pinto beans. I got both because I can fart all I want with you gone. But I guess it never stopped me before. Um.

(The MODELS circle in, threatening. A scary dance, with poses.)

MODELS. Do you know what the old lady said to me the other day after you got on the school bus? "My, she's well-fed, isn't she?" Humiliating.

LEWIS. So. I'm just…sitting here. Surfing photos of badly dressed celebrities. God, this website is SOOOO SLOOOOOOW. I hope these fucking browser vendors iron out their self- prefixing CSS animation stuff soon. Wheeeee. Shoot me.

MODELS. Do I have to put a lock on the refrigerator door? Do I have to ransack your room to get rid of your candy bar stash? Is this what we've come to?

LEWIS. Oh, Ronan tried to use your computer the other day. I found him after lunch clicking around like a ninja. I think he just wanted the bigger monitor. You know, I can't fend off these IT dudes forever, so…

MODELS. If your father were alive he'd be mortified at what you're doing to yourself. You should know that.

LEWIS. So I was thinking like, when you get back? We'll stay late and watch a fuckload of Hulu and eat buckets of hamburgers. But the little ones, the sliders, so I don't have to listen to you bitch about the size of your ass all night.

MODELS. I'm only saying this because I love you. I don't want to see you go through life obese and miserable. The world hates ugly people. How do you expect me to protect you when you won't protect yourself?

LEWIS. Bottom line: I have big plans for us. So hurry back.

MODELS. Tell me how to help you.

Tell me how to help you.

Tell me how to help you.

> (**JESS** *doesn't know how. Freeze on them.*)

> (*Lights up on* **VICTOR** *in the '70s. He is smoking, has many sketches pinned to his wall, and several dress-forms covered in cloth. He is cutting fabric.*)

> (**ESME** *enters. She has gained about twenty pounds since last we've seen her. She holds a large cardboard box in front of her.*)

> (**VICTOR** *barely looks up.*)

VICTOR. Hey. Long time no see.

ESME. Yup. Louella still in your apartment?

VICTOR. Yes.

> (**ESME** *regards the muslin on the dress forms and the sketches.*)

Don't touch those –

ESME. What is this, a pajama pant? A muumuu?

VICTOR. It's in progress –

ESME. You don't have the scratch for these fabrics.

VICTOR. Louella's been helping me. Her church had a fundraiser.

ESME. How *charitable.*

VICTOR. They're nice people –

> (**ESME** *places the box down. We see she is about five months pregnant.* **VICTOR** *finally looks up.*)

No.

ESME. 'Fraid so.

VICTOR. It's not mine.

> *(beat)*

Don't bring this shit to me. You bring this shit to me? Really? I am right in the middle of something fucking massive and you show up with your gut all swollen up like you just ate the fucking sun? What the fuck, Esme?

ESME. Phew. I was worried you wouldn't be happy about it.

VICTOR. Fuck no I'm not happy about it! Was it a money thing? Didn't Doctor Susan say she'd give you a discount on the next one?

ESME. Never even called her.

VICTOR. *(beside himself)* What – okay what the hell is going on?

ESME. I wanted it.

VICTOR. You *wanted* – you're not the only one who gets to make this decision!

ESME. I didn't want you to talk me out of it.

VICTOR. You're not parent-material. *I'm* not parent material.

ESME. What kind of material am I?

VICTOR. Is that a real question?

> (**ESME** *retrieves the cardboard box and drops it on the table before* **VICTOR.** *She begins to dig inside it, showing him various scraps.*)

ESME. Some beat-up military coats from the salvation army, some wicked epaulets, couple rusty belts, some camos, some sliced up T-shirts… I stained a few of them with tea. Put together a book of ideas so you wouldn't have to think too hard…

Oh, and this…

> *(She pulls out a tiny disco ball. Beat.)*

VICTOR. What do you expect me to do Esme?

ESME. I expect you to. To admit. That you see me as something more than a hanger. Or a sidekick. Or a warm hole to slip your dick into whenever the mood strikes.

VICTOR. *You're* the one who abandoned *me.*

ESME. Did *I* invite someone to appropriate your spot in my bed? Did *I* infect our partnership with the bacteria of mediocrity?

VICTOR. You don't give a shit about me Esme, and you don't give a shit about what I want. I've been talking about creating a line that people actually *want* to wear for a year, and it's like you refuse to hear it. You have something else in mind for me. Big fucking ideas. "Victor, go smear feces on a bolt of muslin and sell it to a homeless man." Well guess what. I want to participate in humanity. How about that? I want to be part of a larger fucking conversation, the kind that goes on between normal decent people. Also? I don't want to be ashamed of it. Can you handle that fucking news?

ESME. You wanna participate in humanity. Well you helped create some. Right here. Participate.

> (**LOUELLA** *enters wearing make-up and her hair done.*)

LOUELLA. Oh. I thought she was fired.

> (**LOUELLA** *eyes* **ESME***'s belly.*)

Congratulations!

Would you like a cup of water?

Or some herbal tea?

ESME. *(to* **LOUELLA***)* That man was in Guatamala. His designs *stand for something –*

LOUELLA. *(to* **ESME***)* Victor is under a lot of pressure

He doesn't need to be emotionally taxed.

ESME. *(to* **VICTOR***)* You can stop this from happening. You're not a mercenary. Don't let the need to be loved or, or the feeling that you should be immortal fool you into thinking you're made of something different than you are. You're fucking made of light. And so am I.

> *(long beat)*

VICTOR. They're just clothes.

(Beat. **ESME** *takes her box and leaves.)*

VICTOR. I don't feel well, Louella.

> *(***LOUELLA*** *approaches* **VICTOR** *with compassion, and rubs his shoulders.* **VICTOR** *lights up a cigarette.)*

LOUELLA. I feel so badly for her.
   No job, no family
   And now her looks have gone.

VICTOR. She'll be fine
   She's a strong girl

LOUELLA. You know
   My apartment back home is empty
   She should go live there

VICTOR. In Little Rock?

LOUELLA. A simpler life for sure
   But maybe that's what she needs
   This city is no place for her to raise a baby on her own
   My mother lives right next door
   She would absolutely help out
   She's a firecracker!

VICTOR. I feel so calm when I'm with you. Like nothing bad could ever happen.

LOUELLA. I know.

> *(***VICTOR*** *and* **LOUELLA** *disappear.)*

> *(Lights change. Fashion show!!)*

> *(Projected: "Cavanaugh, 1975.")*

> *(Gorgeous parade in fashions very much of the mid-late '70s: belted chemises in soft food-colored fabrics, pajama pant outfits, blousons, two-piece gore-skirted dresses, giant loose muumuus, and wraps. Also, scarves, hats, and leather accessories. Everything loose, easy, comfy. Simple.)*

(An excellent song from the '70s is heard, probably La Belle's "Lady Marmalade."*)

(Music stops abruptly as **VICTOR** *appears. A* **FEMALE VOICE** *is heard.)*

FEMALE VOICE. And now we turn to the fashion world. Notable denizen of the downtown scene, Victor Cavanaugh has created quite a ruckus with his newest line. Critics have been divided...many feel it bears no resemblance to his previous body of work, while others find it refreshing to have him experiment with more accessible looks. Some are even referring to him as the "Father of American Sportswear." Joining us now in the studio is Victor Cavanaugh. Pleasure to have you here, Victor.

VICTOR. Thanks, thank you.

*(***ESME*** walks by with her suitcase, pregnant.)*

FEMALE VOICE. Why such a radical switch?

VICTOR. Um, well we've been through quite a bit of tumult the past few years as a nation, with the war, and the recession, and et cetera, and I believe it's time to be innocent again and turn our attention to our most basic needs. Comfort. Stability. Simplicity.

FEMALE VOICE. And who would you say is your ideal customer?

VICTOR. Um well one of the nearly twenty-nine million American females in the eighteen to thirty-five year age group. Fashion oriented, but also practical. She wants clothes to complement her busy, casual way of life.

FEMALE VOICE. And, she is willing to pay top dollar for her wardrobe.

VICTOR. Well I believe you cannot put a price on being seen. *Truly* seen. When you de-glamorize the event of the *clothing,* you are creating an event of the *person.* Right?

---

* Please see Music Use Note on page 3

FEMALE VOICE. It's as though you're turning the ordinary into the *extra*-ordinary. A bold move. And it appears to be paying off for you?

VICTOR. Well right now we're, we're just trying frantically to keep up with the demand but frankly it's, the response has been um, overwhelming.

FEMALE VOICE. Kind of heady to go from relative obscurity to international celebrity almost overnight…

VICTOR. Yeah. It's like I'm connected now. Like I'm part of a larger conversation.

ESME. I'm so stupid!

FEMALE VOICE. And how do you feel about this?

VICTOR. Um I don't know yet. Ask me in a few months.

FEMALE VOICE. Ha ha ha. Fair enough. But how do you feel about this?

VICTOR. You just asked me that.

FEMALE VOICE. Ha ha ha. Right, right, fair enough. But how do you *feel* about this?

VICTOR. Um.

> *(beat)*

I don't feel well, Esme.

> *(Now* **JESS** *and* **ESME** *are on stage alone, out of time, for the first time.)*

> *(They sing.)*

ESME & JESS

> THE DIRT BENEATH YOUR SHOES
> THE LINT INSIDE YOUR DRYER
> THE AIR BETWEEN YOUR FINGERS
> THE PAINT UPON YOUR WALLS

> EVERYTHING YOU TOUCH
> BUT NOTHING YOU NOTICE

> HMMMMM-MMMMMM-MMMMMM

> EVERYTHING YOU TOUCH
> BUT NOTHING YOU NOTICE

HMMMMM-MMMMMM-MMMMMM

EVERYTHING YOU –
BUT NOTH –

> *(Song ends abruptly.* **ESME** *disappears.)*

PART THREE

Home

(VICTOR appears with a stack of clothing. Piece by piece he hands each one to JESS. Layered on top of her loose '70s clothes, VICTOR helps to bind her into a difficult, alienating, architectural, Tudor-inspired outfit.)

(LEWIS appears. JESS hears him but does not see him. As she dresses, she listens.)

LEWIS. Um so I figured you're going through some pretty deep stuff, so I made a list. It's called "Freakishly Awesome Things About Jess – The Definitive Index."

(He pulls out his iPad and reads.)

One. How insecure you are.

Two. The way you eat a burrito by piercing the middle first, like you're removing a gallstone.

(VICTOR tightens some ties, some buckles, on JESS's outfit. Gently:)

Three. The way you hurl yourself into pleasure, like. Eating. And fucking.

Four. The way you smell, which isn't a girl smell, it's like sheets and crackers and kombucha and parmesan.

(VICTOR arranges JESS's hair.)

Five. The way you wear the same pair of jeans four days in a row. Thinking no one will notice. I always notice.

Six. The way you sink into your computer with like relief almost. I've never seen someone use code as a life-raft. But you do. I get it. People are a mess, but computers are logic. Logic is incorruptible.

(VICTOR tidies JESS's attire. Just so. Loving.)

LEWIS. Seven. The way you make lists. I make lists. Lists are good.

Eight.

*(Transformation complete. **JESS** is Future **JESS**.)*

Um. That's as far as I got. My battery died. There's other stuff I wanna tell you too. But. Like. Not on your voicemail. So. Bye.

*(He disappears. **VICTOR** unsheathes a lipstick dramatically and hands it to her.)*

VICTOR. Glam it up, Bagel. I'm going outside to smoke.

(He disappears.)

(Lights change slightly…we're in the '70s…)

*(As **JESS** puts her make-up on in a different space. **LOUELLA** enters, wearing **VICTOR**'s casual sportswear, drinking a cup of tea.)*

(Joni Mitchell plays softly in the background.*)

Did you know my hands sew the air in my sleep? Esme told me that once. Sigh. This place. It's getting to me. Sure, it's huge and clean and quiet and junkie-free and a doorman and an elevator and the huge studio downstairs for my work and I'm not working. I hate me not working. Okay so it's only been six months, right? Maybe I'm taking a break. Everyone takes breaks.

You're quiet. Why are you quiet.

LOUELLA. I'm just thinking.

VICTOR. About what?

LOUELLA. My mother.

She and I used to do Music Mondays.

We'd listen to records on my couch for an hour after supper.

Johnny Matthis was our favorite.

I don't know this singer.

---

* Please see Music Use Note on page 3

VICTOR. Joni Mitchell.

LOUELLA. I don't like her.

I feel like she's asking me to feel sorry for her.

I don't like victims.

VICTOR. We're all victims. Of ourselves. Ha ha ha.

(beat)

LOUELLA. Do you think maybe we should…

I think I want to talk about what happened last week.

On Merv Griffin.

VICTOR. Um…

LOUELLA. With the –

VICTOR. Oh.

LOUELLA. I had gotten my hair done. I had gotten my nails done. I wore the most expensive looks from your collection –

VICTOR. It was chaos, I was halfway across the stage before I realized you weren't there… And anyway how many times have you heard me tell people you are the soul of the new Victor Cavanaugh line? Seriously. How many, Esme?

LOUELLA. Louella.

VICTOR. Fuck.

LOUELLA. That's fine. That's great.

VICTOR. I haven't slept –

LOUELLA. In case you needed me to tell you. I wanted to be standing up there in the lights. Next to you. They would have let me on camera if you had said something.

VICTOR. Do not tell me you're so insecure you need to be on *TV* to feel validated. Next show I book, should I drag you up by your hair and plant you right on my cock in front of all of America?

LOUELLA. Victor.

You don't look at me.

VICTOR. I'm looking at you right now.

LOUELLA. Not the way I want you to look at me.

VICTOR. How do you want me to look at you?

LOUELLA. Like you're staring into the sun?

> *(beat)*

VICTOR. I feel like you're punishing me for something I don't understand.

> *(**LOUELLA** stands and grabs her bag.)*

Where are you going?

LOUELLA. Where I always go at 3 p.m. on Tuesdays. Swimming lessons.

> *(**LOUELLA** is about to exit. She pauses at the door.)*

"She's with me." That's all you needed to say.

> *(She exits, leaving **VICTOR** very alone. He turns to look at **JESS**. **JESS** looks gorgeous, glamorous.)*

VICTOR. Ding-ding-ding. It's time.

> *(**VICTOR** hands **JESS** a pair of crazily high heels.)*

JESS. Fuck. Fuck.

> *(**VICTOR** helps her into them. She stands in the crazily high heels for the first time. It's treacherous. Then. **JESS** and **VICTOR** are outside an apartment complex in Little Rock.)*

(to us) We're standing outside the complex. The very spot I stood almost twelve years ago with my ratty duffle bag on my shoulder and a Greyhound bus ticket in my hand. It looks exactly the same. They haven't even painted it.

VICTOR. It's charming, in a disgusting sort of way.

JESS. I can't move.

VICTOR. You can move.

JESS. If I try, my legs will break. Or my body will move toward the door but the rest of me will stay behind.

VICTOR. You look *gorge*. That outfit is *major*. Looks way better on you than it has any right to. And your face is great. All pale and shiny.

JESS. I haven't eaten since Wednesday.

VICTOR. It's working for you. Just try not to look down at your feet or you'll fall over.

JESS. You'll be there to catch me.

> (VICTOR *shakes his head no.*)

You will, though.

VICTOR. I need to get back to New York. I have work to do. I have things to make and things to sell, and people to sell them to. I have to smoke too much and forget to eat and build an empire of clothes to prance in. I have to meet a muse. I have to fall for her in a bad way and then I have to never recover. I have to become immortal.

> (*beat*)

That's all I got, kid.

JESS. Wait. You haven't told me…

VICTOR. Told you what?

JESS. Why…why you never…

VICTOR. …never…?

JESS. Came for me?

VICTOR. How do you know I didn't?

JESS. Because…she said…

VICTOR. I'm sure she said a lot of things.

JESS. Did you?

VICTOR. Does it matter?

JESS. Yes! Yes it does!

> (VICTOR *stares at her. Smiles.*)

VICTOR. Then…

I did.

> (*Long beat as* JESS *contemplates this.*)

See you inside…

JESS. Wait!

> (VICTOR *blows smoke and vanishes.* JESS *panics.*)

JESS. *(quietly)* Help.

Help.

> *(No one comes.)*

(to us) It might be enough, right? To just stand here? Make my peace with the exterior of the building? I say this knowing she is inside somewhere waiting for me, her only child. Knowing that I'll scour the hedge for the one odd rock, under which I will detect the spare front door key. I will use it to open the door and I will be immediately thwacked with the aroma of old cigarettes, moldy carpet, and dog pee. The smell of my youth.

> *(beat)*

> **(JESS** *places an unlit cigarette awkwardly between her fingers. Finds the key under a rock.)*

And I unlock the front door.

And I walk up the long uneven flights.

> *(This walk becomes a fashion show of sorts.)*

(quietly, to herself) Believe you are the most rare creature on the planet...

You ARE the most rare creature on the planet.

Don't look at your feet!

> **(JESS** *places her hand on the doorknob. She opens the door. A shriveled* **ESME** *lays on the couch, eyes closed, covered in afghans and wearing a plastic nose tube.)*

Momma?

I'm wearing high heels.

> **(ESME** *does not respond.* **JESS** *touches her.)*

You're so small.

You finally lost the weight.

> *(sudden banging on the door)*

> **(JESS,** *terrified, says nothing.)*

*(More banging. **ESME** pops up in bed and rips out
the nose tube. She is not old, as previously thought.
She is in fact younger than **JESS**. And quite
chubby. She wraps herself in an afghan and grabs
JESS's cigarette. She lights it.)*

VICTOR. *(through the door)* I just want to see her, Esme. You
could go into the other room if you want. I won't even
hold her. I might hold her.

　　*(**ESME** smokes.)*

(through the door) I'm on national television talking
about how some bitter woman in Arkansas won't let
me see my two-year-old daughter and you know what?
Everyone thinks it's a tragedy. Except you.

Please.

　　(Beat. She lets him in.)

ESME. I knew you were coming. Louella's mother told me.
Can't keep her mouth shut. I'm surprised you drove,
though. It's a long way from the Upper East Side. You
look like shit.

VICTOR. I quit smoking.

Louella's gone.

ESME. I heard. The old lady won't shut up about it. Moved
in with some lawyer, right?

VICTOR. No idea. You –

ESME. I'm fat.

I eat whatever Jess won't. Pizza, french fries, hot dogs,
gross foods little kids are supposed to love. But she
only wants carrots and peas. She's so gorgeous, Victor.
A fucking angel. And you should see her clothes. She
picks them out herself. She's going to be a stunning
model. It's all she talks about. Parades around in my old
shit, swinging her little hips around…

VICTOR. And you have nothing to do with that.

ESME. Nope. She's a natural. And she's SO SKINNY. The
doctor says she's underweight.

VICTOR. Where is she?

ESME. Louella's mother is watching her. That woman has posture like an elbow macaroni –

VICTOR. Why did you send her away?

ESME. Because you were coming.

VICTOR. That was cruel.

ESME. I thought we might have some catching up to do. How's New York?

VICTOR. Fuck you.

ESME. And work?

VICTOR. Fuck you, Esme.

ESME. Glad to hear it. Does every cheap Cavanaugh rip-off that flies through the sewing machine of some toddler in China remind you you're not a man any more?

VICTOR. Come back. Just come back.

ESME. Work for it.

VICTOR. I need you.

ESME. Say "Every cheap Cavanaugh rip-off reminds me I'm not a man any more."

VICTOR. I'm not a man anymore.

ESME. The whole thing.

VICTOR. "Every cheap Cavanaugh rip-off reminds me I'm not a man anymore."

ESME. And why would we leave this perfectly livable city? Everyone is really nice. Jess loves it here.

VICTOR. She's two, she doesn't know any better.

ESME. Garage sales and lemonade stands. This adorable apartment. Those watercolors. Louella Wilkens originals!

VICTOR. Esme. I don't think you understand. How desperate I am.

ESME. Oh believe me. I do.

> (**ESME** *moves her afghan to reveal her attire – a cheap knockoff of the Cavanaugh line.*)

It's very comfy.

No dry cleaning

A little give in the waist.

And it doesn't make my ass look huge.

VICTOR. *(quietly)* Where did you get that?

ESME. Dillards.

On sale.

> (**VICTOR** *is decimated.* **ESME** *smiles coldly.*)

You're immortal.

You can die now.

> *(long beat)*

VICTOR. Okay.

> (**VICTOR** *vanishes/commits suicide.*)

> (**ESME** *turns to* **JESS**. *Lights a cigarette. Vicious.*)

ESME. Fuck you, Jessica

You half-sack of wet cement

You half-eaten cream puff

What's in that duffel bag, twelve pounds of turkey grease?

To suck on during your bus ride east?

Sure you don't want some fucking congealed bacon fat to go with that?

Or a lard sandwich?

Oh, sorry, you ARE a lard sandwich.

You pathetic pile of shit.

Look at what you did.

You ruined yourself.

If your father were alive?

He would be DISGUSTED BY YOU.

Everything I ever did I did for you

And you just leave me here to rot.

So fine.

Happy eighteenth birthday, you ungrateful bag of garbage.

ESME. *(cont.)* Go get on that Greyhound bus.

Have fun in New York.

Have fun being a fat sack of crap.

Have fun never having a man want to fuck you.

Have fun being alone.

> (**ESME** *settles back onto the couch, covers herself with the afghan, and replaces the nose tube.*)
>
> *(looong beat)*

JESS. *(to* **ESME***)* It's really beautiful out. Unseasonably warm, they keep saying. It's the kind of day where every person steps foot out her door inhales in unison and feels like crying a little. Hats and gloves thrown into purses or in backpacks for the evening, but not for the day… the walk to the subway, the walk at lunchtime, pumpkins on doorways and spicy hot drinks and cider, too many apples…

But the seventy degrees is the thing that kills. You walk down the leaf-coated street and you think of the one person whose lover you should have been. You think of jumping into a pile of leaves with him in Central Park, though never in your adult life have you jumped into a pile of leaves and especially not in Central Park where there could be rats lurking beneath and CERTAINLY not in your horrible fall coat that's one loose thread away from disintegration…but anyway today there are no rats and coats don't fall apart and the air is meant for eating and strangers are there for you to touch yes that lady with the beautiful knee-high brown leather boots and the chocolate corduroy skirt is yours and yes the man with the square-toed shoes and the Times folded beneath his arm blowing on his coffee waiting for the light to change he is yours too.

> (*The* **MODELS** *gather around* **JESS** *to hear her tell her story. They are dressed as G.I. Jezebel. As fantastic and outlandish and godawful as* **ESME** *had described.*)

JESS. And your lover, the one you never had…he's lying in a pile of leaves around the bend.

> (**LEWIS** *appears. Seems to be waiting for the phone to ring.*)

His arms are outstretched. He's waiting for you. And just for a second, everything is as it should be.

And maybe I don't actually hate myself, mom? I think maybe I inherited that from you?

So um…you can take the hate back. All of it. I'm done with it.

> (*She goes to her mother's closet…reams of beautiful clothes, all designed by* **VICTOR**, *none of which would fit either of them.*)

> (*She takes the beautiful architectural and flowing gown. Page 26 of* **VICTOR**'*s Fall '71 Lookbook. Autumn and spilled mimosa and butt-sex and laughter. And lays the gown on* **ESME**'*s body.* **ESME** *looks more beautiful than we've ever seen. The* **MODELS** *lift her body and exit.*)

> (*Beat.* **JESS** *takes off her shoes. Dials her phone.* **LEWIS** *answers.*)

JESS. She was in a coma when I got here. Died last week.

LEWIS. I'm so sorry Jess.

JESS. I'm okay.

> (*beat*)

LEWIS. Um, where's your perv?

JESS. Turns out he was made of pixels after all.

LEWIS. Oh. Weird. Are you coming home now?

JESS. Yes.

LEWIS. Good. You sound hungry.

JESS. I am.

LEWIS. We'll go get Mexican. On me.

> (**JESS** *smiles. Blackout.*)

End of Play